Success in Social Studies
Student Workbook

GRADES 2-3

PAT-DENE CONNELL

Aligned to New York State Standards
2018

Fulton Books, Inc.
Meadville, PA

Published by Fulton Books 2018

ISBN 978-1-63338-434-7 (Paperback)
ISBN 978-1-63338-435-4 (Digital)

Printed in the United States of America

This book is dedicated to my beloved sister,

Margaret Doreen Gaskin.

Contents

Introduction

This book is based on the new New York State social studies curriculum for grades 2 and 3. It covers major concepts associated with the Common Core Social Studies Framework for these grade levels.

A focus on poetry can help students connect to key social studies material. The format will create greater student engagement with nonfiction texts and deepen their retention skills.

The tasks included will help develop students' word knowledge and provide ground work for deeper discussions and inquiries. In addition, these tasks will provide ways to practice writing responses in other content areas as students closely read and extract information to support their responses.

My Notes

SECTION I

Communities

What is a community? A *community* is a group of people living in the same place; their lives are similar in many ways.

Types of Communities

Urban

Suburban

Rural

An Urban Community

In an *urban community*,

people, often with several things in common,

tend to live in one location.

They play and work together,

which benefits everyone.

Urban communities or large cities

have many buildings and busy streets.

People from all backgrounds

and races can be found in

residences and businesses.

A Suburban Community

A *suburban community,* is located outside the city,

with apartments and houses, both big and small.

Some people may live apart from others

in buildings that are not skyscraper-tall.

People enjoy a blend of city and country life.

Schools, hospitals, and police, and fire services

all help to make life enjoyable for everyone.

A Rural Community

A *rural community* is not like the city.

It has farmlands and open spaces,

fewer people, and many natural areas

with butterflies, moths, and beetles.

There are many things to do there:

You can fly a kite,

ride a bike,

or even go fishing.

Q1: In the spaces below, write two things that people do in each community:

Urban

a._____

_____

_____

b._____

_____

_____

Suburban

a._____

_____

_____

b._____

_____

_____

Rural

a._____

_____

_____

b._____

_____

_____

Q2: Read the poems again, then use the Venn diagram to write what is similar or different in any two communities.

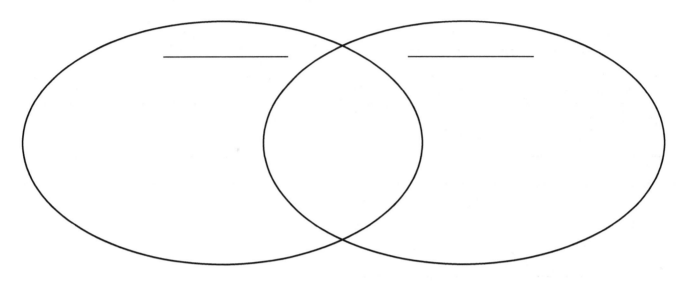

Q3: Do you live in an urban, rural, or suburban community? In the space below, write two things you can do in your community.

I live in _____ community. Two things I can do in my community are _____ and _____.

Drawing Activity 1

Directions: Draw and color one feature of each community below.

Urban

Suburban

Rural

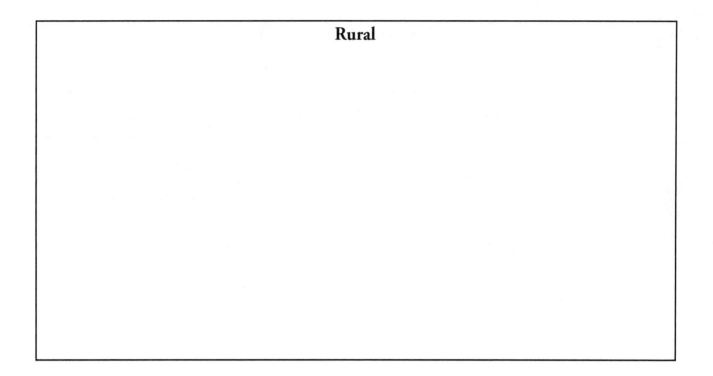

Culture

People in urban, suburban,

and rural communities

are not all the same.

Some speak different languages

and are called by different names.

Living together is exciting.

Everyone learns from one another.

What makes a community special

is its diverse culture.

Q1: Think of one activity in your community that includes everyone. Write it in the space below.

In my community, everyone _____.

Democracy

Democracy: A form of government in which people are free to choose their leaders.

Freedom: The power or right to act, speak, or think without breaking a law.

Our country is a democracy;

we have rights and responsibilities.

We vote to put leaders in place

to govern and keep us safe.

We must show respect for authority

and enjoy our freedoms

in our democracy.

Q1: What is a democracy?

_____

_____

_____

Q2: According to the section above, what is one freedom people have when living in a democratic place?

_____

_____

_____

Human Rights: Rights all humans are entitled to.

Prejudice: A preference or dislike for one trait over another such as race.

Human Rights

Governments in communities around the world

make laws to keep people safe,

but there are often struggles

with inequality and race.

Citizens and governments

have to protect human rights.

They have to fiercely fight

unfairness and prejudice.

Q3: What are human rights?

_____

_____

_____

SECTION II

Rules and Laws

Rule: A guide that one can follow.

Law: A rule made by the government.

Citizen: A person who is legally a member of a particular country.

Civic-Minded: Doing things that help a community.

Rules are set by people
so that things can run smoothly.
It is important to obey them.
to prevent chaos or injury.

As good citizens, we must agree
to obey the laws of our community.
A person may face a fine or imprisonment
if he or she chooses to disobey.

We must be orderly
at home, at school, and in public,
in groups large or small.

We should all try to be good citizens.

To be civic-minded

is to understand that we are responsible

for our homeland.

Voting or running for public office are

examples of civic-mindedness.

Q1: How is a rule different from a law?

_____

_____

_____

Q2: Give an example of a good citizen as described in the poem.

_____

_____

_____

Q3: Read the poem again. Underline the words that explain what happens to a person who disobeys the law.

Q4: Circle the examples that show how a person can be civic-minded in his or her community.

Think. Create. Write.

Directions: Create **one** rule for your home and **one** rule for your class. Write in the spaces provided.

My Home Rule

_____

_____

_____

My Class Rule

_____

_____

_____

Community Helpers

We must take the opportunity

to say thank you to our community helpers,

such as postal workers, paramedics, police, and firefighters.

They are like our sisters and brothers.

They travel throughout the neighborhood

for the common good.

Adults can be volunteers

and give service when they can;

in school or other places,

they can lend a helping hand.

Q1: Who are some community helpers?

_____

_____

_____

Q2: Why are they important?

_____

_____

_____

Drawing Activity 2

Directions: Draw, color, and label two community helpers in the space below.

My Notes

SECTION III

Geography and Natural Resources

Geography: An area of study that deals with the locations of countries, cities, rivers, mountains, lakes, and more.

Resource: A useful item that is natural or made by human hands.

Challenge: A difficult situation or a problem.

To find a community,

we use a map or globe.

There are special symbols or legends

that give information

or show us where to go.

There are natural resources

that help us decide where to live.

Land and water and forests

all have benefits to give.

Not all communities have the same

resources.

In world communities, there are many challenges,

such as lack of space, overpopulation,

droughts, and pollution.

People modify their environments

to suit their daily lives.

They may build bridges and parks

or grow crops and raise livestock

in order to survive.

People also adapt to their environments,

for there are things they just cannot change.

In the wintertime, they wear special clothing,

and in the summertime, they do the same.

Q1: **How do people modify their environment?**

_____

_____

_____

_____

Q2: **Write one way you can adapt to your environment.**

_____

_____

_____

_____

Continuity and Change

Some communities change from time to time.

New ideas, technology, and different behaviors

can bring about changes in a culture.

Events in the past can be traced back

by future generations

using evidence in maps, pictures, writings, or

even artifacts.

Some communities continue traditions

They like to celebrate important events from the past

using art, music, dance, and literature

to share their rich history and culture.

Q1: **Why do some communities change?**

_____

_____

_____

Similarities and Differences in World Communities

Communities across the world share similarities.

Families and schools engage

in common activities and have similar rules.

They may have different languages, religions, or holiday celebrations,

but their activities help each community

share its **unique** identity.

Q1: How are world communities similar?

_____

_____

_____

Q2: How are world communities different?

_____

_____

_____

Q3: Explain what the word *unique* means in line 6.

_____

_____

_____

Challenges Communities Face

Resources are not the same in every place.

Some areas have malls and large supermarkets,

but are animal-and farmland-free.

These areas have to rely on rural places

to get the resources they need.

Other challenges can also be the cost

of goods and services,

or shortages of resources

in some places.

Lack of space and change in weather

are also problems some communities must

face together.

Q1: **According to the section above, what are two problems some communities have to face?**

_____

_____

_____

_____

Drawing Activity 3

Directions: Draw and color a picture that shows one challenge a community faces.

Interdependence

People in communities depend on each other

to provide food, clothing, and shelter.

Having basic needs

helps communities succeed.

Goods are items that we buy.

Services are done by people with special talents and skills.

Often, we have to pay for them

with money that we earn.

When people buy things,

they often check the prices

to see if they are reasonable.

If the prices are high, they'll often buy less,

but if prices are low, they'll often buy more.

Q1: **In what way do people in communities depend on each other?**

_____

_____

_____

Q2: **According to the poem, why do buyers purchase more of a good?**

_____

_____

_____

Taxes

Taxes are extra money charged on goods.

They help keep our communities strong.

They finance services for the old and young

and help make the community safe for everyone.

Taxes pay the salaries of government workers,

such as police and firefighters.

This money helps in so many ways

to make each community a better place.

Q1: **Why are taxes important?**

_____

_____

_____

_____

Student Writing Task

Question: Which community do you prefer to live in? Give details from the text to support your answer.

Beginning - Introduction

```



```

Middle - Body

```



```

End - Conclusion

```



```

Name _____ Class _____ Date _____

Question_____

_____

_____

_____

_____

_____

_____

_____

_____

_____

_____

_____

_____

SECTION IV

Review Activity 1

Directions: Reread Section 1, then complete the crossword puzzle below. Use the letter clues to figure out the correct word.

PART 1

Across

3 An area at the edge of a city[s]

6 Something that people have to obey [r]

7 Something that a person cannot do without[n]

Down

1 An area in the country[r]

2 A set of rules that everyone must obey[l]

4 Something that people ought to be allowed [r]

5 An area in a town or city [u]

Review Activity 2

Name _____ Class _____ Date _____

Directions: Review Sections 2 and 3 then complete the puzzle below. Use the letter clues to figure out the correct word.

ACROSS

2 Something that is a problem [c]
7 Of a special kind [u]
8 To change slightly [m]
9 Something people have to obey [r]
10 To make something suitable for a new purpose [a]

DOWN

1 Money paid on a good or service [t]
2 A group of people who share the same interest [c]
3 A set of rules people must obey [l]
4 Something that can be used [r]
5 Map key [l]
6 Ball-shaped map of the world [g]

Review Activity 3

Directions: Find the following social studies concepts in the puzzle below.

CHANGE	CITIZEN	COMMUNITY	CONTINUITY	DEMOCRACY	ENVIRONMENT

GEOGRAPHY   INTERDEPENDENCE   LAW   NEED   RESOURCES

RIGHTS   RULE   RURAL   URBAN   WANTS

```
I  N  T  E  R  D  E  P  E  N  D  E  N  C  E
Z  C  O  Z  L  Y  W  A  N  T  S  U  D  E  G
V  G  O  A  C  A  K  H  D  Y  E  S  W  N  Z
W  I  R  N  A  Q  O  G  C  C  Z  S  T  V  K
F  U  D  U  T  C  H  A  N  G  E  S  Y  I  U
R  D  L  A  G  I  R  X  S  L  I  C  X  R  R
G  J  X  C  O  C  N  T  T  Q  L  S  G  O  B
E  B  J  C  O  M  M  U  N  I  T  Y  T  N  A
O  N  O  M  E  Z  H  O  I  O  H  E  O  M  N
G  V  E  L  K  J  L  A  W  T  T  R  J  E  F
R  D  U  V  L  I  V  M  N  W  Y  X  B  N  O
A  R  E  S  O  U  R  C  E  S  Z  I  R  T  M
P  E  N  M  C  J  X  L  E  F  S  C  O  Y  C
H  Q  I  J  T  L  X  G  D  R  I  G  H  T  S
Y  D  C  W  L  R  F  U  C  I  T  I  Z  E  N
```

My Notes

About the Author

Pat-Dene Connell is a National Board-certified teacher and a graduate of Teachers College, Columbia University. She is a public school social studies teacher and was inspired to write this social studies workbook because of her love for poetry and the interest and excitement her students display when reading poems.

Ms. Connell likes listening to music, playing the violin, and writing. Her favorite poets include Thomas Gray, William Wordsworth, and Derek Walcott. She is the author of other children's workbooks, including *The Miracles Activity Book* and *The Parables Workbook*.

She hopes that the poetry in the text will make social studies content more appealing to young learners as they are introduced to new concepts and vocabulary.

CPSIA information can be obtained
at www.ICGtesting.com
Printed in the USA
LVHW060434310320
651715LV00017B/2475